Sausages!

By Anne Adeney

Illustrated by Roger Fereday

Special thanks to our advisers for their expertise:

Adria F. Klein, Ph.D.
Professor Emeritus, California State University
San Bernardino, California

Susan Kesselring, M.A.
Literacy Educator
Rosemount-Apple Valley-Eagan (Minnesota) School District

PICTURE WINDOW BOOKS
Minneapolis, Minnesota

Levels for *Read-it!* Readers

- Familiar topics
- Frequently used words
- Repeating patterns

- New ideas
- Larger vocabulary
- Variety of language structures

- Challenges in ideas
- Expanded vocabulary
- Wide variety of sentences

- More complex ideas
- Extended vocabulary range
- Expanded language structures

A Note to Parents and Caregivers:

Read-it! Readers are for children who are just starting on the amazing road to reading. These beautiful books support both the acquisition of reading skills and the love of books.

The RED LEVEL presents familiar topics using common words and repeating sentence patterns.

The BLUE LEVEL presents new ideas using a larger vocabulary and varied sentence structure.

The YELLOW LEVEL presents more challenging ideas, a broad vocabulary, and wide variety in sentence structure.

The GREEN LEVEL presents more complex ideas, an extended vocabulary range, and expanded language structures.

When sharing a book with your child, read in short stretches, pausing often to talk about the pictures. Have your child turn the pages and point to the pictures and familiar words. And be sure to reread favorite stories or parts of stories.

There is no right or wrong way to share books with children. Find time to read with your child, and pass on the legacy of literacy.

Adria F. Klein, Ph.D.
Professor Emeritus
California State University
San Bernardino, California

First American edition published in 2005 by
Picture Window Books
5115 Excelsior Boulevard
Suite 232
Minneapolis, MN 55416
877-845-8392
www.picturewindowbooks.com

First published in Great Britain by Franklin Watts, 96 Leonard Street,
London, EC2A 4XD

Text © Anne Adeney 2002
Illustration © Roger Fereday 2002

Printed in the United States of America.

Library of Congress Cataloging-in-Publication Data
Adeney, Anne.
"Sausages!" / by Anne Adeney ; illustrated by Roger Fereday.
p. cm. — (Read-it! readers)
Summary: A poor man conspires with the village shoemaker to play a trick that will pay
for a new pair of shoes.
ISBN 1-4048-0645-8 (hardcover)
[1. Wagers—Fiction. 2. Shoemakers—Fiction.] I. Fereday, Roger, ill. II. Title. III. Series.
PZ7.A261135Sau 2004
[E]—dc22
                                                                          2004007331

Once there was a poor man named Albert who needed some new shoes.

Albert asked the village shoemaker to make him some fine new shoes.

But when they were ready, Albert couldn't pay for them.

"It's clear that you don't have enough money to pay for these shoes," said the shoemaker.

"But I know how you can pay, and it won't cost you a penny," he added with a smile.

9

"How?" asked Albert.

"From now on you must only say one word: *Sausages!*" the shoemaker told him.

"You must not say anything else
until we meet again!"

"Sausages!" agreed Albert, and he
hurried home.

"You're late," grumbled Albert's wife. "What have you been doing?"

"Sausages!" replied Albert.

"What did you say?" she asked crossly.

"Sausages! Sausages!" Albert

shouted, trying not to laugh.

Albert's wife was worried. She
rushed next door to ask her
neighbor for help.

"Come quickly!" she yelled.
"There's something wrong
with Albert!"

The neighbor hurried next door.

"What's wrong, Albert?" she asked.

"Can I get you anything?"

"Sausages!" came the reply.

"He's lost his mind!" wailed
Albert's wife.

"I'll fetch the mayor," promised
the neighbor. "He might help!"

The mayor came to visit Albert.

"What's the problem?" he asked.

"Sausages!" replied Albert.

"What?" shouted the mayor.

"Sausages!" Albert said again,

feeling very silly.

Soon, the whole village knew that there was something wrong with Albert—he could only speak nonsense! Albert was embarrassed.

The next day, the mayor visited

the shoemaker.

"Have you heard the news?" asked the mayor. "Albert has gone crazy!"

"Nonsense!" replied the shoemaker.

"He has!" said the mayor crossly. "He only says 'Sausages!' when you talk to him! He makes no sense!"

So the shoemaker played his little trick. "I'll bet you 50 gold coins that Albert is not crazy," he said, knowing the mayor was rich.

"It's a deal," agreed the mayor,

and they went to find Albert.

"Hello, Albert!" said the shoemaker.

"Sausages! Oh, I am pleased to see
you!" answered Albert. "Now I don't
need to say 'Sausages!' any more.

The whole village thinks I'm crazy
because of this sausage talk. These
shoes have certainly cost me a lot!"

"Not as much as they've cost the mayor!" the shoemaker laughed, as the mayor handed him 50 gold coins.

So the shoemaker was paid for his shoes after all. Now Albert pays his bills on time. And the mayor has never made a bet again!

Levels for *Read-it!* Readers

**Read-it! Readers help children practice early reading
skills with brightly illustrated stories.**

Red Level: Familiar topics with frequently used words and
repeating patterns.

I Am in Charge of Me by Dana Meachen Rau
Let's Share by Dana Meachen Rau

Blue Level: New ideas with a larger vocabulary and a variety
of language structures.

At the Beach by Patricia M. Stockland
The Playground Snake by Brian Moses

Yellow Level: Challenging ideas with an expanded vocabulary
and a wide variety of sentences.

Flynn Flies High by Hilary Robinson
Marvin, the Blue Pig by Karen Wallace
Moo! by Penny Dolan
Pippin's Big Jump by Hilary Robinson
The Queen's Dragon by Anne Cassidy
Sounds Like Fun by Dana Meachen Rau
Tired of Waiting by Dana Meachen Rau
Whose Birthday Is It? by Sherryl Clark

Green Level: More complex ideas with an extended vocabulary
range and expanded language structures.

Clever Cat by Karen Wallace
Flora McQuack by Penny Dolan
Izzie's Idea by Jillian Powell
Naughty Nancy by Anne Cassidy
The Princess and the Frog by Margaret Nash
The Roly-Poly Rice Ball by Penny Dolan
Run! by Sue Ferraby
Sausages! by Anne Adeney
Stickers, Shells, and Snow Globes by Dana Meachen Rau
The Truth About Hansel and Gretel by Karina Law
Willie the Whale by Joy Oades

**A complete list of *Read-it!* Readers is available on our Web site:
www.picturewindowbooks.com**